HAPPY BIRTHDAY
WORD BIRD

by Jane Belk Moncure
illustrated by Linda Hohag

THE CHILD'S WORLD

MANKATO, MN 56001

Library of Congress Cataloging in Publication Data

Moncure, Jane Belk.
  Happy birthday, Word Bird.

  (Word Birds for early birds)
  Summary: Word Bird learns about the twelve months
of the year as he tries to figure out when his
birthday will be.
  [1. Birds-Fiction.   2. Months—Fiction.
3. Vocabulary]   I. Hohag, Linda, ill.   Title.
III. Series: Moncure, Jane Belk.   Word Birds for
early birds.
PZ7.M739Hap   1983   [E]   83-15256
ISBN 0-89565-256-0 -1991 Edition

HAPPY BIRTHDAY
WORD BIRD

JANUARY

2	3	4	5	6	7
9	10	11	12	13	14
16	17	18	19	20	21
4	23	24	25	26	27	28
29	30	31			

"Is my birthday in

January?" asks Word Bird.

"No," says Mama Bird.

"January is the time for snow...

and snowballs and a snowman."

"Is my birthday in
February?"

"No," says Mama.
"February
is the time for

valentines

and candy hearts."

"Is my birthday in March?"

"No," says Papa Bird.
"March is the time for

shamrocks

and baseball

and kites."

		APRIL				
						1
2	3	4	5	6	7	8
9	10	11	12	13	14	15
16	17	18	19	20	21	22
23/30	24	25	26	27	28	29

"Is my birthday in April?"

"No," says Mama.
"April is the time for

showers

and
bunnies

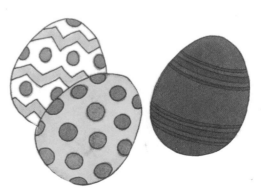

and eggs."

MAY						
	1	2	3	4	5	6
7	8	9	10	11	12	13
14	15	16	17	18	19	20
21	22	23	24	25	26	27
28	29	30	31			

"Is my birthday in May?"

"No," says Mama.
"May is the time for

flowers

and
Mother's
Day."

"Is my birthday in June?"

"No," says Papa.
"June is the time for

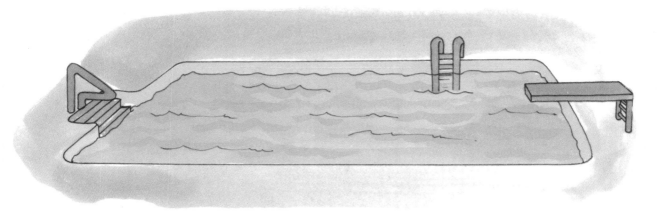

swimming
pools

and Father's Day."

"Is my birthday in July?" asks Word Bird.

"No," says Papa.
"July is the time for

parades

and fireworks!"

"Is my birthday in August?"

"No," says Mama.
"August is the time for

picnics

and fishing."

"Is my birthday in
September?"

"No," says Papa.
"September
is the time for books

and pencils

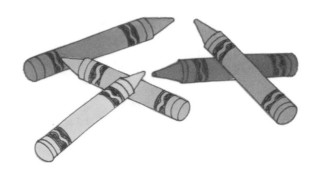

and
crayons

and a
lunchbox."

\octicon	\octicon	O C T O B E R				\octicon
1	2	3	4	5	6	7
8	9	10	11	12	13	14
15	16	17	18	19	20	21
22	23	24	25	26	27	28
29	30	31				

"Is my birthday in October?"

"No," says Mama.
"October is the time for

jack-o-lanterns

and Halloween spooks."

NOVEMBER

			1	2	3	4
5	6	7	8	9	10	11
12	13	14	15	16	17	18
19	20	21	22	23	24	25
26	27	28	29	30		

"Is my birthday in November?"

"No," says Papa.
"November
is the time for
Indians and Pilgrims

and Thanksgiving pie."

"Is my birthday in December?"

Can you guess what
Mama and Papa said?

"SURPRISE!"

"Happy Birthday, Word Bird."

Can you read these words with

Word Bird?

January

February

March

April

May

June

July

August

September

October

November

December

When is your birthday?